SYMPHONY OF EMOTIONS

SAURABH GUPTA

Copyright © 2020 by Saurabh Gupta

This is a work of Poetry. Names, characters, businesses, places, events and incidents are either products of the author's imagination or used in a fictitious manner. Any resemblance to actual persons, living or dead, or actual events is purely coincidental. All Rights Reserved

First Edition: December 2020

Typeset in Book Antiqua

ISBN: 978-93-90267-40-8

Cover Design: Prashant Gopal Gurav

Publisher: StoryMirror Infotech Pvt. Ltd.
                145, First Floor, Powai Plaza, Hiranandani Gardens, Powai, Mumbai - 400076, India

Web: https://storymirror.com
Facebook: https://facebook.com/storymirror
Twitter: https://twitter.com/story_mirror
Instagram: https://instagram.com/storymirror

Dedication

This book is dedicated to all the readers and everyone who supported my journey leading me to where I am today - becoming a published author.

A big and sincere thank you to everyone

Acknowledgement

I would like to extend my sincere gratitude to the entire team at StoryMirror Publications, especially to my indefatigable editor, Ms. Divya Mirchandani, who is as cool-as-cucumber and the trustworthy founder, Mr. Bibhu Datta Rout. All of them have been a wonderful support. My gratitude to Mr. Meet Jain who facilitated everything smoothly through several rounds of fruitful discussions..

I also wish to express my heartfelt appreciation to everyone, who enriched me with love and care and fortified me through the vicissitudes of life.

Preface

This book is the natural outcome of my undying passion and interest in poetry. I always have been curious about languages, its vocabulary and interweaving of words that emerge into captivating rhyming schemes, its forms and genres, the romantic and modern arrangements, the mystery behind the origin of thoughts and all the expressed and unexpressed emotions involved. This book contains poems of different genres and is suitable for all age groups; something everyone can relate to; a different perspective on life for both the initiated and uninitiated readers.

I've often found myself transported to different time periods and locations, envisioning myself in different situations, wondering what it would have been like to be present and experience it first-hand, to be able to express and portray the sentiments precisely. The poems have been penned down during travels, daily commute, lectures; at workplace, and at almost every other common place that you can think of - 'me time' in the nights, parks, the college canteen to mention a few. The topics span across the diversity of emotions that everyone goes through while living all his life for people around him; they are very relatable to a common man. I hope the readers will be able to connect with me, 'live' my emotions and feel the same sense of gratification I felt placing them into words. The poems in the book have been written with a lot of heart in it and it is intended to be read from the heart. While some poems smoothly fell into place in a matter of few minutes, the others were the result of a month's long labour. I promise, upon reading, you will go through a roller-coaster ride of emotions, making you feel excited, happy, motivated, disappointed, sad or even desperate, all at the same time.

Contents

Appreciate

Everywhere around the world, a fight is underway,
For excelling, not by doing better,
rather pulling back others they meet on their way,
Envy others, but never hate,
Kindly open your heart and appreciate.

You are good at your own things,
No one can take away your wings,
You too will fly one day; it is never too late,
If you open your heart and appreciate.

Pause for a moment in this fast- forward life,
Whilst being with yourself, be away from the strife,
Stop, take a breather, 'You are doing well',
let this note reverberate,
But also open your heart and appreciate.

Desperation will lead you nowhere, belief will
Be ready to stumble before believing in yourself,
you know the drill,
Expressing gratitude is the need of the hour,
so begin without await,
You have to open your heart and appreciate.

A thank you note on one's wishes,
on one's status, a smiley face,
Resonates the emotion despite the distance,
making a moment of glad grace,
Replying a thumbs-up on one's achievement is entitled
enough, not difficult, you need not elaborate,
All you need is an open heart and a heart to appreciate.

The world will certainly be peaceful,
more beautiful than it is now,
Persevere and finish once you start,
but make a start somehow,
Be kind, be humble, generous enough, no matter what,
acknowledge, there's more to life than always being
disconsolate,
Raise a toast to life, celebrate,
and whole heartedly appreciate...

Unparalleled Bond

People connect but never so quick,
Like a sorceress, you triggered a magic trick.
Your voice too gentle, your graceful fumble,
Like a serene reflection, you were too humble.

The way you talked, the ease you brought,
An hour's time felt way too short.
Days went by, the conversation became long,
In no real time, the connection felt strong.

If a hundred thoughts brought chills to spine,
You were a part of some ninety nine.
We gelled well, reciprocated well,
sun started to shine upon us,
Everything seemed to fall in place, and was perfect, thus.

No wonder, it's often heard that happiness is a myth,
The moment you smile comes the devil,
standing tall like a monolith.
Overwhelmed by anguish, engulfed in pain,
I now feel chronic,
True to the core is the phrase often iterated, 'Life is ironic'.

Though not around,
you have been in my thoughts all this while,
With you, I definitely can walk my last mile.
I will not shy down to express the emotions that I behold,
These emotions are something that the world
needs to be told.

Dream in the Hindsight

I began my journey with a dream in the hindsight,
Always with the hope that everything,
one day, will turn out right,
Whoever I met on the way kept asking the same thing,
"Who am I, what new to the table do I bring?"

I kept hustling, kept the blood gushing through the veins,
With a smile on my face, I kept tussling the pains,
I kept speaking to my heart which all the way used to sing,
"Patience is your virtue, patience is the king".

To an extent I imbibed this belief, I became carefree,
Settling for what came my way, I became a new me,
Misunderstandings became a part and
parcel of everyday living,
It gradually bothered less; and I resolved to forgiving.

Time has changed; my patience shall anyway die,
Leaving every mess aside,
I just want to spread my wings and fly,
Fly away, far away, from where none could find me nor
could one see,
Where I could not be recognized, not even by me.

Living with fear has always kept me aloof on the cliff,
With a lot to ponder about the future, always surrounded
with 'buts' and 'ifs',
For once I want to shed every thought out and
not just act tough,
I want to shout out to the world once and for all,
that I have had it enough.

To live this thought deep breathes I take,
I generally close my eyes,
Trying to feel better I do get a ray of hope mixed with sighs,
I sleep with this hope that, everything one day,
will turn out right,
Only to realize the next day, that the journey was in
itself a dream in the hindsight.

She

She is a girl, she is a peer,
Amongst all, she is her father's dear,
She is a wife, she is a mother,
She is a prepossessing soul; unlike her, there's none
another.

Though every day is there for her to celebrate,
But more so for the others to think and reverberate,
Have we done enough for them in this archaic world?
A question that every now and then gets hurled.

A woman unarmed, need not seek revival,
She should not smother;
neither should she worry for her survival,
An epitome so unreal is blurring her eyes away,
It is time that we give them intent, a hope, a ray,

Give them their space, let them fly high,
And they'll be an unstoppable force,
so much so that even the sky goes shy,
Mince your steps towards this change and
let them collate the courage,
Give them a word of your mouth that you'll always
encourage.

Today on woman's day, let us pledge this initiative,
Support vehemently and let them be creative,
Sit back, relax, for glory let them thrive,
And see them overcoming the struggles of life.

Brave Face

On the outside, I may be smiling,
On the inside, the struggle you'll never get to know,
Regardless of how inexplicably hard it is to hide,
The feelings such sustained I'll seldom show.

It may happen that nostalgia hits us hard,
that I hope it does,
It may happen that we cross paths again, that I hope we do,
It may happen that all our commemorations come alive,
that I know we will experience,
However, it is also certain that I'll not be the one who you
once knew.

What may have entrenched in the days gone by,
Doesn't always transpire the time in the future that we
seize,
Though it is difficult to part from my humanly soul,
I'll walk through my fated path with one impeccable ease.

The atrocities I'll pen; I only have gratefulness to offer,
I'll let you be untroubled as there's nothing to me
that you owe,
On the outside, I may be smiling,
On the inside, the struggle you'll never get to know.

Fragments of Life

Underwhelmed we live a life so pretty,
Valuing the futile as much is unfailingly a pity.

Drive your will through, look beyond your curse,
Live fragments of life thankfully, lest it shall be worse.

Care and concern stand bygone,
It is time to separate the pros from the cons.

Unpredictability in life resembles an unrhymed verse,
Untangle the predicaments indebtedly,
lest it shall be worse.

What in life did you bring, what from life will you take,
Putting rest aside over self is certainly a mistake.

One life is what you get, there is no time to rehearse,
Belittle the miseries gracefully, lest it shall be worse.

You will be pushed down more often than
being pulled along,
Never dishearten, but catapult yourself with
the force that won't prolong.

Wear a smile on your face and put it on recurse,
Live fragments of life thankfully, lest it shall be worse.

I, an Introvert

Not many words I say; yes I am quiet,
Feelings I hold back, stopping them from authoring a riot,
Fighting to be free from the world's girt,
Yes, I am an introvert.

I distinctively will say what I have to,
Assuredly not when you want to,
Neither one needs to assess me, nor have me assert,
Yes, I am an introvert.

I don't mind being a hunted fugitive,
Some will let me be myself, while some will be intuitive,
I will not be subdued, I definitely won't feel disconcert,
Yes, I am an introvert.

Abundance of patience I hold, don't push me enough,
Embrace the humble me, it's hard to act tough,
Plenty of emotions run through my veins, I am not inert,
Yes, I am an introvert.

I have my own world of words to read from and write to,
I don't shy away from doing the little things that I do,
These make me happy, I don't always have to exert,
Pleased to say, that yes, I am an introvert.

A Silver Lining

A deadly disease or a deadly sin,
To make this end, we have to begin.
Begin our solace in the most discomfort,
Start slow with a small spirited effort.

Step up to the task and not step aside,
Control your anxieties and just stay inside.
It may be difficult, no one said it may not be,
But that's the only way for us to be free.

You call it corona or 19-COVID,
Standing together in unison will surely make it timid.
We all are in this together, even without hand in hand,
Let us show the world how tall we stand.

Time to be a soldier, a soldier for our motherland,
No recognition, but the reward around this is for us to
understand.
No protecting the borders, no use of artillery,
Hospitality to an Indian is no hidden mystery.

Sing your heart out, dance to the weirdest beat,
Sketch with the little ones, take the driver's seat.
Play games together, revisit the old times,
Do all the little things that ring the melancholy chimes.

Spend time with your loved ones in this phase so hostile,
Be optimistic and live life every day with a big bright
smile.
Life is a gift and life is at stake,
Don't give it away, savour it, whatever it may take.

Unconditional Love

She wakes up early,
She sleeps late,
She in no condition will complain,
She'll give your dreams the much needed weight.

She is tough, she is inspiring,
She is innocent, she is sweet,
She is ever so trustworthy,
No matter how far she is,
we must oblige her with a morning greet.

She will make your presence surreal,
She will drive away all your fear,
Her love is such indisputably unconditional,
That she will not let your eyes drop a single tear.

Besides all the affection she offers,
We, at times, do take her for granted,
So much so that we bother less to even talk to her,
In spite of all, her care remains selflessly implanted.

Everything said and done for her is way less,
Avoid putting the relationship with
your mom through any test,
She will never turn her heels on you,
Her endearment is by far the purest.

Respect, honour, money, loyalty, friends,
All that one urges for may be earned the hard way,
What can never be earned is mom's love,
do get that straight,
Love her back unconditionally before it is too late.

Await

You were the expressions that he waited patiently for,
From the annoying child in him, to the smile that he wore,
You helped unravel all his hidden mischiefs,
You were the rarest gift from his small list of wishes,
which he deliberately tore.

A thousand pleasures gleamed in him with
your voice so sweet,
Having you around was, certainly to him, a treat,
There is plenty in the hindsight that he reminisces,
You were the rarest gift from his small list of wishes,
which had to take backseat.

He has a secret that he has kept all this while,
He started staying happy, making his own dream aisle,
He was finding reasons to make you stay for
just a little longer,
You were finding one to move away, meanwhile.

Standing outside the reach of the sound and
sight to which he would once obsess,
He finds a world out of his world that he has yet to
impress,
Parting away from the rarest gift he once wished for,
He awaits this new world to wholeheartedly express.

First Love

The morning vibes, the classroom jibes,
The tale of our love perfectly describes.
When you knew that I was looking at you,
Cause your eyes were searching for me too.

The breakfast preaching, the professor's teachings,
Despite the rush our eyes greetings.
When you knew that I was waiting to come to you,
Cause that's what you were waiting to do too.

Break was the time that we eagerly looked up to,
Coffee vending machine was the place to head to.
When you knew what I will like to have to,
Cause that's what you said you liked too.

Happy were the days that we had spent together,
I now wish the time had stopped there and forever.
When you knew that I used to look at you,
And I knew your eyes were searching for me too.

Rise Above

Everyone is running their own mental race,
With a grimace sometimes, or with a smirk on their face,
Battling hardships in their own merry ways,
Some hoping for peaceful nights,
while some for glory days.

Gruesome thoughts bewilder the mind,
Seventy years in democracy and here we are, still confined,
Happiness, humanity, compassion, all an illusion,
The senses do not lie, it is not a mere delusion.

Be done with feeling tired,
be done with feeling secluded,
Be done with putting a full stop,
be done with being concluded,
Confrontations will never be easy,
they'll test you against all odds,
The orchestra was ever ready,
you just need to choose your chords.

You did not give up, instead you chose to fight,
You have battled the darkness until you saw the light,
Unwind your miseries, be the glimmer of hope,
For those who are helpless, but are willing to cope.

Some people are not so lucky, though some do survive,
Raise your voice, for your experience, is ear worthy,
don't place it in archive,
One life saved is like saving the whole of humankind,
Emotions thus obtained, will be the best you'd ever find.

Mental illness though not a choice, but recovery is,
Put this feeling in one's head, as they were his,
Let their demons be conquered,
for have them achieve their quest,
Gather their unpleasant thoughts and put them to rest.

It's now time to speak up, it's now time to speak out,
Let people come to know what this illness is about,
You have to stop the stigma,
you have to break the silence,
It's high time now, that we end this violence.

Take a Smile

How about starting the day with a smile?
How about making an impression of walking through a
glorified aisle?
How about giving life a chance in an environment so
hostile?
Let living turn out to be an experience,
an experience worthwhile.

How about having all your happiness compile?
How about moving forward, yet be proud of your
achievements erstwhile?
How about walking pass stress with
an exemplified guile?
Let living turn out to be an experience,
an experience worthwhile.

How about respecting every being, is he wilful or docile?
How about conforming to all religion,
is he Jew or gentile?
How about raising alarms against hypocrisy and
crimes by juvenile?
Let living turn out to be an experience,
an experience worthwhile.

How about repudiating million thoughts spread
across a mile?
How about relaxing and avoid thinking for a while?
How about making living an experience,
an experience worthwhile?
Just as we began let us end the day with a smile.

Unforgiven

The surroundings so ordeal,
There's nothing much I feel,
From your heart my heart's omission,
Just unforgiven.

My world without you, I never envision,
Tyrannical life lessons were available for revision,
In the blink of an eye,
you became my non-acquired acquisition,
Just unforgiven.

Fighting with me was I, a war of attrition,
Dreams froze and so did I,
with my thoughts undergoing nuclear fission,
The distance with you broke me with absolute precision,
Just unforgiven.

From walking beside to walking apart was
your solemn decision,
Losing you gave me nothing but my inhibition,
From your soul my souls excision,
Just unforgiven.

An Honest Expectation

An honest faith I have,
In the expectations that I behold,
This is another phase my dear,
The story is yet to unfold.

Together, forever are not mere words,
They are the feelings that I live,
For all the mistakes that may be made,
I'm living in the hope that you forgive.

From meeting as strangers,
Till talking as friends,
Then loving unconditionally,
All the feelings that we comprehend.

Something seems missing now,
Wait, wait, and wait all around,
Itching, scratchy heart all the way,
Frustration, irritation is all that surround.

Mood swings getting worse,
More control I need, but don't know how,
The one who made you feel special yesterday,
Is making you feel unwanted now.

No matter how much I get hurt,
Can't change what my heart says,
I want you in my life,
And I want you in all the possible ways.

An Agonizing Year

It's been a year since we last met,
Though I'm smiling, my heart is still wet,
With all the pains in the world,
The toughest is having you as my intangible asset.

I have survived so far, and will survive ahead,
I'll keep my promises; and tears I'll not shed,
But I'm bound to have some moments so numb,
Where I may get killed by a fine thread.

I wish I had you for the rest of my life,
I wish I hadn't had to struggle, or for you I had to thrive,
For you are the happiness that I could ever wish,
These wishes are the reason for me to be alive.

From before the sunrise, till after the sunset,
From the flashbacks while I'm awake,
to the dreams that I get,
You occupy every inch of my mind,
Even though it is been a year since we last met.

Faded

I desired to lose me from your sight,
That is how I have dreamt all my nights,
I desired to wake in the manner so same,
That is how my life I did frame.

The thought got stronger, my conscience gave a shout,
I wished someday, somehow you heard me out,
What else could be said in chorus and rhymes,
Which had already not been said a thousand times.

I may seem to be the quintessential guy so tough,
The day is not too far, when I have had it enough,
I won't mind walking past you, be it difficult, howsoever,
Silence will be my weapon, and smile will be my power.

The desire seems dying; the frame left incomplete,
Leaving behind me, with myself to compete,
Hallucinating I was, may be thinking that
you need me as I did,
Believe me, I want nothing of the past redid.

Until We Meet Again

Excited I was to meet you again,
In the midst of the cloudy mountains,
With your presence around me I had,
Nothing to lose, but everything to gain.

Your awesome smile, your amazing charm,
Your childlike behaviour, your holding my palm,
Your joyous laugh, your cheerfulness,
Did bring me a lot of calm.

I travelled, we met; everything was at such ease,
Together we lived some special memories,
Days went by, and so did you,
Leaving behind a picture in which your hand I seize.

The special memories of you,
Will always bring a smile,
If only I could have you back,
For just a little while.

Then we could sit and talk again,
Just as we used to,
You always have meant so very much,
And will continue to do too.

The fact that you are not with me anymore,
Will always bring about pain,
But you're forever in my heart,
Until we meet again.

Only if a Heart could Speak

It was one fine day,
When I met this beautiful girl.
Very cute, very pretty,
Simple, adorable like a pearl.

Not realizing where we were heading,
I tried talking, being the unusual me.
She complimented and comprehended,
Understanding me, was her great USP.

Slowly and steadily I felt for her,
Though scared to confess.
She made me comfortable and helped me be me,
And brought all the feelings out that I suppress.

We talked more, we walked more,
We started spending time together.
A lovely phase we started sharing,
In the hope that we stayed like this forever.

Sadly the time arrived when we had to bid goodbye,
And it all happened too soon.
All we could then do was to pray,
That we meet again on one pretty moon.

I miss you and I know you miss me too,
I can feel the love so strong.
This very day I promise to you,
That nothing between us can go wrong.

I wish I could talk till the end of day,
But as usual I'm out of words, and you already know.
This roller coaster ride of emotions stays incomplete
without what I often say,
I love you, more than what I could show.

Within You

Within you, is the reason to live every moment in time,
Within you, the life I want is always mine,
Within you, I have an immaculate friend so divine,
Within you, I see myself at cloud nine.

Within you, the chaos around me sounds like a melody,
Within you, enjoying my life becomes a necessity,
Within you, I have peace, there is no animosity,
Within you, I find my life's perfect recipe.

Within you, the crowd presents a charming ensemble,
Within you, I get a head so humble,
Within you, I have played the best gamble,
Within you, I know I always have a hand,
if ever I were to tumble.

Within you, all my imperfections seem perfect,
Within you, my entire wish list seems checked,
Within you, my life certainly seems far from being
wrecked,
Within you, I have found a friend so perfect.

Incomplete

Like an incomplete you, an incomplete me,
You and I were not meant to be.

Like an adolescent is unaware of all the anxieties,
pretentiously carefree,
You and I were not meant to be.

Like how a river feels that could never enter the sea,
You and I were not meant to be.

Like a wanderer captivated for years in chains,
unable to flee
You and I were not meant to be.

Like a lock and its misplaced key,
You and I were not meant to be.

Like the presence of a moon on an eclipsed night be,
You and I were not meant to be.

Like an innocent's unheard plea,
You and I were not meant to be.

Like the rainbow from the clouds that never escaped free,
You and I were not meant to be.

Like the seedling that never grew into a tree,
You and I were not meant to be.

Like an end which none could foresee,
You and I were not meant to be.

You were always my happy place to be in,
you will always continue to be,
It's just that you and I were not meant to be.

Broken Strings

You pulled me closer, you pushed me away,
You are the reason that I feel this way.

With you, life was a dance, an endless ballet,
Suspended in time, and then swept away.

From waiting to talk for a minute on your birthday,
To remembering the dates that we met without fail,
but alas, anyway.

I played my part with full conviction
which no one could replay,
Only to realize I was going to be in a disarray.

Shallow-hearted you became, a little difficult to weigh,
The sky broke out on me in red dismay.

It's too late for the tears to shed, or for me to pray,
I hereby call it out aloud a doomsday.

The path was never expected to be a child's play,
However, it may have been,
but now this is all that I could say.

That I love you, though it's so cliché,
There is nothing else that is left for me to say.

You pulled me closer, you pushed me away,
You are the reason that I feel this way.

Life Goes On

Somewhere, someday, I want to meet you again,
Until then I don't want to stay the same,
With new priorities on my mind,
I want to live my life without disdain.

I will keep your memories in me so alive,
Having you in my subconscious mind, I will survive,
May you be happy in whatever you do,
But for you, my dear, I will never thrive.

For your smile, I will wait no more,
For my eyes will not ail, whilst staring at the door,
For your soul in my soul is so enthralled,
You are already submerged in me to my core.

Longing for my happiness, I'll continue to smile,
Hiding behind my sorrows, I'll continue to walk the aisle,
May be life is not as insane as it seems,
By living every moment without you,
I'll continue to live for a while.

The Missing Link

Missing the air, missing the sky,
Missing the water, everything is dry.
No one to hear, no one to listen to,
Missing the you, missing thy I.

Missing the way, missing the desire,
Missing the flight, missing the fire.
No one to be seen, no one to catch an eye,
Missing the you, missing thy I.

Missing the words, missing the irony,
Missing the dialect, missing the symphony.
No one to hold on to, no one to rely,
Missing the you, missing thy I.

Missing the life, missing the hold,
Missing the love and the story to be told.
No one to care, no one to set relief a sigh,
Missing the you, missing thy I.

Life, Love and You

Life is eternity, yet is confined
Life is uncovered, yet is blind
Life is love, love is you,
Every instance with you, I swear, is déjà vu.

Life we desire, yet we despise,
Life we acknowledge, yet we compromise,
Life is love, love is you,
Let's travel together, just me and you.

Life is favourable, sometimes inopportune,
Life is susceptible, sometimes immune,
Life is love, love is you,
Carrying hopes and wishes all the way through.

Life is diminishing, though can prolong,
Life is lyrical, though an imperfect song,
Life is love, love is you,
Your presence bewitches my smile to accrue.

Bidding Adieu

The hardest time in friendship,
Is when it is time to say goodbye,
Though I wish I could make you stay for just a little longer,
I have to let you go, for you to touch the sky.

I have cherished our times together,
I'm craving for something that I could do,
I hoped that it would have lasted forever,
Nevertheless I have to bid my goodbye to you.

Now we will be far gone,
The air that surrounds will no longer sing for you,
The song we hummed will only announce the dawn,
Today, our stories will begin anew.

Life is not a destination,
and has to be enjoyed while you travel,
There's no doubt if you'd make it through,
I just want you to know and never forget,
I will surely miss you.

Listen to your heart whenever caught in a dilemma,
My only advice to make your dreams come true,
And I hope that someday we meet again,
For each day I will pray for a tomorrow with you.

Safety – Time to Introspect

Caring for one, caring for all,
If we think is not a big call,
Incidents do happen unrehearsed,
So let us begin with safety first.

Safety is not an expression, or a lesson that can be taught,
Although if ignored, it does hurt a lot,
Are we actually safe? On this question let us introspect,
Health and Safety is for sure an important aspect.

There is no stopping to unforeseen events,
Avoidable they are, all it needs is for you to be the ferment,
As a reform preludes a movement,
it doesn't always require one to be at the helm,
If nothing more, your act will certainly give a smile to you,
a smile to them.

Safeguarding oneself and those close to you
doesn't require much,
A little bit of awareness and a small spirited effort as such,
The time is perfect for us to take the baton,
Don't be oblivious and wait for the things to
automatically happen.

Let us be proactive, let us be intolerant,
Let us imbibe this feeling and let us complement.
Let us not quaver, rather raise our voices in unison,
When one is safe, then safe is everyone.

My Prized Possession

I want you to be there for me,
Through good times and bad,
I know I can count on you,
To be there when I'm sad.

Life without you,
Just wouldn't be right,
I wouldn't be able to get through,
Each day and night.

When I've had a bad day,
I want you to be only a call away,
When life takes that crazy turn,
I want you always to be there to help me learn.

I want to have many good memories together,
I hope we remain friends forever,
No matter where we are,
I know we'll never be too far.

You're presence, your charm is such my friend,
We can be together till the very end,
Even when we're old and grey,
I want you to be here still, to help me get on my way.

Entreat

Losing my temperament,
Losing my mind,
Look into my eyes when I say this,
Without you, I'd rather turn blind.

No one I want to see,
No one I want to hear,
It's you, it's you the only one,
Who I need, yes, I need very near.

Dizzy is my day,
And so is my night,
You being not around,
Is my biggest fright.

Getting amateur day by day I am,
In my poems, in my behaviour,
The sudden silence is haunting me,
Please set it all right, my saviour.

Every moment spent together still seem so fresh,
In the wink of an eye, I can live them, in and out,
Just like another wink clears it all,
With droplets of water finding their way, shouting out loud.

I don't know how we are supposed to be,
All I'm doing is making efforts to be not like me,
Hurting is a small word to explain how much it hurts
to be like this,
Let me care for you once again, and you can be carefree.

Guilted Inhibition

For an instance we did share a glance,
I was there and I had a chance,
I could have saved a life yesterday,
If I had not chosen to part my way.

For the rules that are knowingly unknown,
He left few lives all on their own,
I could have saved a life yesterday,
If I had called out aloud a hey.

For the mournful misery that he left behind,
Following the path to a petition unsigned,
I could have saved a life yesterday,
If it wasn't for a split delay.

For closing my eyes was a decision unwise,
He was taking a risk which lead to his demise,
Filled with this guilt I never had to stay,
If I would have saved a life yesterday.

Seeing people taking risks with their mind break,
Unalarmed to the situation that their health or life
will be at stake,
Put up a question right away,
To help them live another day.

Perceiving a danger and walking away,
Is a hideous act in its own way,
With this, I hope you never have to say,
I could have saved a life yesterday.

Happy New Year

All my wishes choose your joy,
New Year is here for you to enjoy,
Accept new beginnings with open hands,
With every passing second, let your smile expand.

Acquaintances are temporary, connections are permanent,
Of utmost importance is to convert the impertinent,
With New Year knocking on the door,
Wishing connections and perseverance at your shore.

May you find happiness in the happiness of others,
As life is full of intricacies where you may have to stutter,
You may not get everything in the form you desire,
Take it as a blessing as something beautiful might transpire.

Contentment, gaiety, and cheerfulness is for you to get,
Believe in the Almighty as He has this pattern set,
Relax to the core and let your worries destroy,
New Year is here for you to enjoy.

Ask Yourself

Is it really difficult for someone to give you their time?
A question over the years you mysteriously ponder,
A few minutes is what it takes, a common feeling,
That's no big mountain to climb, or a maze to wander,

They say they were occupied,
leave it upon you to understand,
You never doubt them though,
despite the delay being forever,
A few words is what it takes;
a light hearted conversation is what you foresee,
That's no goal for you to endeavour, however.

It is their time, it will always be,
You are no one to set their things right,
A few thoughts shared is what it takes,
though it is for them to acknowledge,
That's no worry for you nonetheless,
you need not cling too tight.

Patience is a virtue, you are never entitled to leave it,
But is it worth the wait;
is it worth experiencing a cliff-hanger?
A few days, a few months,
a few years it may be, or it may be a lifetime,
If worthy enough, express vividly to the least,
don't hold on to your anger.

Why do you take it upon you to empathize always,
an expectation to understand,
Neither you may, nor should you ever mind,
that is not no crime,
Untroubled you be, be carefree,
stop asking yourself this question,
Is it really difficult for someone to give you their time?

Always

Always a 'Hi' there is, to begin with,
then a pause to see if ye connect,
Your earnest waiting, he reciprocating, talking daily,
then gradually a pattern will follow,
All goes well until one fine day
when he sits back and registers,
Without the hurt, the heart is hollow.

You wanted to talk your agony out,
you wanted a friend so unreal,
Having him hand his heart out to you,
you ended up having his soul.
Unalarmed to the consequence,
never trying to decipher the mystery,
Though you only wanted a piece,
he instinctively gave you his whole.

Your calming presence dispersed in the blink of an eye,
Leaving him reeling with the emotions thereafter.
Chaotic he became with nothing much to hold on to,
If not for the memories unprocessed,
he managed to survive by a whisker.

With years gone by, his heart and mind decided to call a
truce, he moved on, though only in his feet,
You, however, may find his essence exactly
where you eclipsed.
Despite all, he still stands firm on his choice even now,
The promise of support with emotions unmixed.

He knew that you always looked out for a James Potter,
Unthoughtful of the Snape,
who vehemently wants to wait for nights and days.
'After all this time?' when asked by anyone,
He invariably wants to reply with an 'Always'.

Be a Voice

Influenced we are from the day of our birth,
There is no superior being than us,
none in true sense of worth.
The others are only there for us to use,
Howsoever beneficial, be it by care or by abuse.

Research conducted in laboratories, causing them pain,
New born puppies and kittens drowning in the rain.
Caged, often beaten for entertaining in circus,
Choked up with tears, left alone to die like rotten carcass.

They go through so much but never do they complain,
This gives us no right to treat them with disdain.
They are innocent beings; they barely have a choice,
They too have feelings; they aren't toys.

Each day we come across articles about horrors imposed
upon them,
Ending up playing the blame game,
we are quick to condemn.
We pretend that we care for them,
but do we really practice what we preach?
Take one step forward so that you widen your reach.

Animals too have a life of their own,
Neither let them weep, nor let them moan.
You will surely see,
how the world would smile and rejoice,
Stand up for them, and if not more, just raise your voice.

Black Lives Matter

It's all in the head, which differentiates,
No country is oblivious to it, be it India or be it the States.
Maligning people on caste, on creed, on colour,
Is a sin, nothing to be proud of, do get that straight.

Belittle your egos and look beyond one's body,
You are no superhuman just because
you can afford an Audi.
You certainly cannot keep this masquerade for long,
No wrongs in boasting your perfection, but never
underestimate an ordinary shoddy

Who gave you this power to discriminate,
the senator, or the Lord himself?
Well, if you believe so, cut across your forehead, as a
useless antique above it, is not even worthy of the shelf.
You are yet to be nurtured and watered like a bud,
Even though you have grown in size, there is something
up there that is smaller than that of an elf.

Everyone in this world has their individual liberties,
With none such liberty of eluding others from their
opportunities.
Opportunities to shine, opportunities to rise,
opportunities to make a merry world of their own,
Let's stay united, irrespective of our belonging to
different communities.

Going forward, let us pledge, there will be no white,
and certainly no black,
Let this echo on the streets as loud as the rifle's crack.
Make it so loud that even the deaf join you in your triumph,
And those deafer, in their white shirts black trousers,
can just relax and sit back.

We will stand against this prejudice,
there is invariably no debate,
For everyone living somewhere somehow
will have the same fate.
Some will be buried, while some will be reduced to ashes,
For all are equal when you enter beyond God's gate.

All the Best

It feels like yesterday that you started your career,
With everything uncertain, with everything unclear,
Far away from home, hustling through the crowd,
Heading towards a life, so unfamiliar.

You have been resilient, you have been tough,
Living all alone, a path that was rough,
Moving ahead, you had to take some decisions,
Some were thoughtful, and some you had to bluff.

You have become strong, you are now independent,
Hope that you always stay in the ascendant,
This is a journey for you to enjoy,
Pedal to accelerate and achieve what you intend.

Tomorrow is a new beginning at your behest,
Another opportunity to prove that you are better
than the rest,
Whenever your feet wobble,
look for a shadow just behind your back,
The shadow will always be praying for your best.

Farewell

Farewells are often hard,
End of an era in the same yard,
Together we have seen all the ups and the downs,
Together we have managed to smile through the frowns.

There is plenty that I need to say,
But I am out of words today,
With this opportunity, may your fortunes touch sky high,
In the hope that we'll meet soon, I for now will say a bye.

Emotions today are on the rise,
Bringing numbness to my eyes,
I've always heard people saying,
he's a brother from a different mother,
Only to realize it all along the time while we were together.

With your presence no more around me,
will certainly leave a void,
It is hard to accept this,
but something's are which one cannot avoid,
One constant support I will miss with your presence not
around me,
Bidding you farewell, but only momentarily.

Unfolding Friendship

To the friendship anew,
I lend an open hand to you.
However, it is for you to decide,
How do you want us to pursue?

If one is an introvert from the outside,
The adored company, he is often denied.
It is when one goes beyond, closer to the heart,
Is when one gets the unfeigned you, yet untried.

I'm ready to take that step, provided you agree,
Solemnly I promise to your beside I'll always be.
No special thing you'll be required to do,
Just be your original self, lively, smiling, and carefree.

A relation so true in the future with you I behold,
Hoping it to be there till we grow old.
Leaving everything on you to ponder and answer,
Our story is yet to unfold.

A Blissful Camaraderie

It was our destiny or my fortune,
To meet you one day, to meet you soon.
To be spending days together forever,
From morning till the pretty moon.

Then came rushing down my mind a thought,
Shall I call you a friend or shall I not?
Why not, my heart asked,
In this dilemma, I got caught.

Slowly and steadily our friendship will flourish,
I hope I oblige with some moments that you cherish.
With no idea of our future, I will go ahead,
Keeping in mind the time we embellish.

Today is special, yes definitely it is,
For in this dark tunnel you came as a bliss.
I know I can look up to you and so can you,
I hope we live this journey all the way through.

Your easy going ways mean that
I'm blessed with no agony,
With peace and joy and the merrier harmony.
Your presence around me is what I always pray,
I hope our friendship shimmers in every possible way.

Nothing Like Before

A feeling of nostalgia surrounds me now,
Living I am, but don't know how.
Giving myself a chance to head solo,
Pushing against the limits here I go.

A force so strong holding me back,
Held on to the ground, an intent I lack.
Swallowing the pain and the agony I am,
But it feels as if you don't give a damn.

Irritating instructions, restrictions is all I hear from you,
Harsh it is, so rude,
hurting like if an arrow just got through.
There's a storm that is gushing through my brain,
If I bleed it out, it would take a lifetime to stop the rain.

This is not the way I feel to make it normal,
It is rather getting more and more formal.
No more morning messages, no more night calls,
Keeping away is like fighting with myself
in a roadside brawl.

When I walk, I see you,
When I play, I feel you,
When I talk, I need you,
Even though I am here, but I can't find you.

No demands I have, I'll create no nuisance,
At least keep me in your thoughts for once.
I will not bother you, and for you I won't even thrive,
I'll simply live mine and let you live your life.

One small wish is all I have ever expected,
To be the first person in your mind rather
than being neglected.
For sharing, for caring, for loving,
even though not as lovers,
But maybe doing the same things as best friends forever.

My Wish for You

The day has finally arrived,
Marking the end of the vigil you survived.
Duh!! I'll just cut the crap and switch to ground rule,
To bid you farewell, let's go old school.

Your distinct laugh, your testing bay fights,
Your ever so vibrant personality
will no longer be in sight.
Your addiction to food, our intellectual talks,
and the ultimate after lunch tea,
Will be missed most by me.

Some common friends first and now that you'll go,
Will go all the sane sense in this place, that you owe.
Adorable, sweet, caring persona that you carry,
Will definitely be a blessing to the person you marry.

With new relationships coming your way,
Please don't let old friendships turn grey.
Wishing you all the luck in your endeavours ahead,
You'll be missed is way small a feeling to be aforesaid.

A Proud Mentor

Sitting at the office desk,
I was striking the computer keys,
When I was introduced to my mentees.
There was a hush; suddenly there were people all around,
And then there was you, silent, unmoved,
footed to the ground.

New to the job, new was the place,
people unknown and a mysterious mentor,
One who could sense your fright,
and that you had a lot on your plate to wonder.
Luckily you had your friends alongside,
Your helping hand, your shoulder, your guide.

It was a struggle initially, everybody does see this phase,
The phase that only marks the beginning of better days.
You kept the fight on, you grew in confidence,
You became an integral part of the team's confluence.

A big thank you, for all the patient listening,
A big thank you, for bearing with my mood swings,
truly unconditioning.
A big thank you, for being a friend more than
being a mentee,
True to the words I've often said,
you'll always have my support, I guarantee.

And finally today, you successfully have got used to the
corporate mess,
Learning how to address everybody, despite all the stress.
It is now time for you to take on new flights,
All my wishes to you, may you achieve unmeasured
heights.

Stay humble, stay calm, stay just the way you are,
Don't worry even if you stumble, just reach out,
I am not too far,
Like it has always been and shall be for evermore,
I will always and happily be your proud mentor.

Good Old Days

Holding tight to the feelings,
I will pour my heart to you,
My presence may be a little too small,
I'll remember the time, I'll remember us all.

I never could have imagined,
This year will end this way,
Nothing to leave behind,
Everything to take away.

The friendship, the bonds,
Could not have been that strong,
If it was not you standing right behind,
To make the others feel that they belong.

Whether it was low, or it was high,
Whether one was happy or whether one cried,
You were there, carrying a sense of care that sees no end,
Without any demands, you all stood beside your friends.

An amazing experience you guys endured to me,
It started with I, which soon became we,
Contentment, gaiety, joy, happiness, you all brought,
You all, as one big family, simply rock.

Take Me Away

Take me away for better days,
Where we see the landscapes amidst the haze,
Take me to this place,
Where soundlessness of nature brings us solace.

Take me away for better days,
With nothing to worry about, nothing to chase,
Take me to this place,
With everything to run at our own pace.

Take me away for better days,
Where the ocean is calm, the sun sprinkling kinder rays,
Take me to this place,
With horizon in sight, certainly a frame to embrace.

Take me away for better days,
Where there is you, where there is I,
where our heart stays,
Take me to this place,
Where there is only love and care to showcase.

Take me to this place,
Where we are free,
of our whereabouts we have left no trace,
Where we stay forever together, beyond the greys,
Take me away for better days.

A Heart's Vision

You tend to see only that can be seen,
Little do you read through the lines between.
By the time you realize the damage may be done,
You may want to speak, but to be heard now,
you may have none.

"What you see, is what you believe", the eyes often say,
"Not necessarily true", the heart shall convey.
You feel distracted by the commotion thus caused,
With numb eyes, heavy heart, feeling shuddered,
trembled, paused.

The heart, though small, expresses at large,
It is simply not a place where you can barge.
It has no sight, but can see beyond opacity,
When it comes to expressing, it knows no capacity.

With full conviction, it unabatingly sheds love,
Disregarding any hurt, the agony, the pain, it rises above.
The eyes can weep, thus feel better;
but this cannot be leveraged by the heart,
It continues to care until torn apart.

Surpass the line of sight, trust the heart,
see what is untold,
The heart speaks louder when the lips are on hold.
Love needs no voice, it is unconditional,
invariably inevitable,
You only have to see beyond what is visible.

Green Life

For new beginnings we often urge,
End your sleep waiting; it's time to emerge,
Go all out, without worrying about what you could lose
as there is no in-between,
Go ahead, the path is green.

You may lack courage, you may lack experience,
It's only a matter of one positive step,
spot the tiny hindrance,
Take strides outside your comfort zone,
as no one has ever seen,
Go ahead, the path is green.

Envying is often taken as a feeling so negative,
How you perceive this emotion hence
becomes imperative,
Envy others, never hate, make shadows with
your own sheen,
Go ahead, the path is green.

If you don't succeed, never curse your luck,
What will eventually pay one day is your hard work,
Absorb the tranquillity, take up new things,
always be keen,
Go ahead, the path is green.

As existence is important to you, so it is for nature,
The heart that it offers is no mystery to any creature,
We will always be in debt of it,
we could only oblige by keeping it clean,
Go ahead, the path is green.